KU-350-015

TROUBLE WITH BRUFF

0 7217 0023 3
First impression 1967
Second impression 1968
Third impression 1970
Fourth impression 1972
Fifth impression 1972
Sixth impression 1974
Seventh impression 1975
Eighth impression 1976

Printed in England by
Henry Garnett & Co Ltd,
Rotherham and London

TROUBLE WITH BRUFF

by PETER YOUNG

Illustrator VERA CHADWICK

Editor George Robb, M.A.

SCHOFIELD & SIMS LTD., HUDDERSFIELD

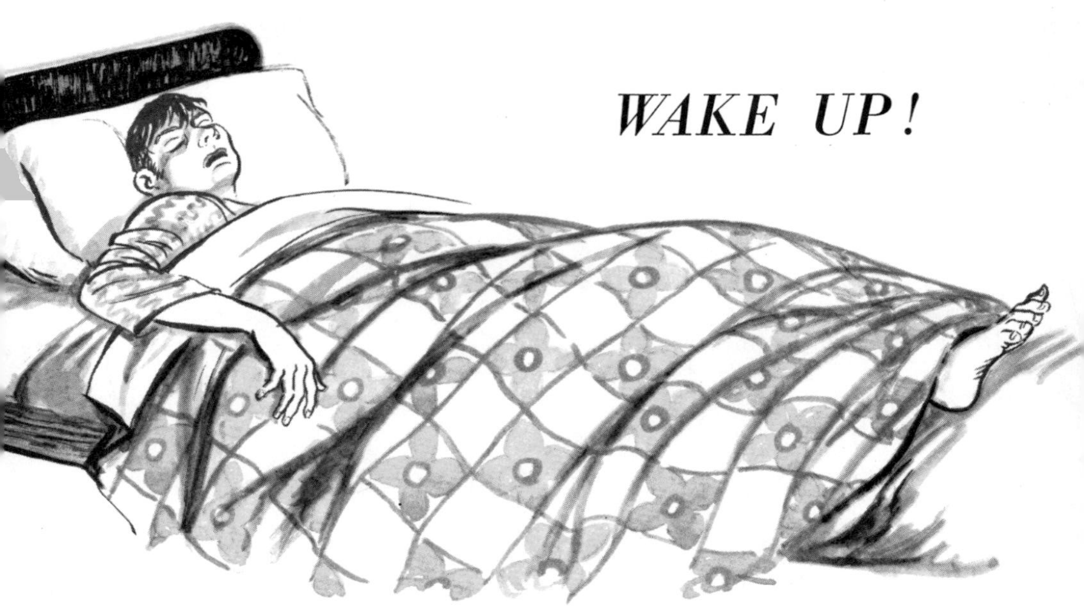

WAKE UP!

Jerry Raven woke up with a start.

He listened.

A snore came from his brother, Rod. Jerry knew Rod's snores had not made him wake up. He was used to Rod snoring.

He listened. The alarm-clock by his bed ticked on. It was ten to six.

Then he heard the sound again. It was the bark of a dog.

"Bruff!" exclaimed Jerry, in alarm.

He leapt out of bed. A book fell from his bed to the floor. He picked it up. It was called "HOW TO TRAIN DOGS".

"I must train Bruff to-day!" Jerry said to himself.

Jerry threw on his clothes as quickly as he could. Again he heard Bruff bark. Jerry knew that if Bruff woke up his father there would be trouble.

Jerry didn't want trouble.

Jerry was used to trouble. He was always getting into it. But now he had Bruff. All his life he had wanted a dog. Most of all he had wanted a boxer dog. Yesterday he had got his dog. He had got Bruff.

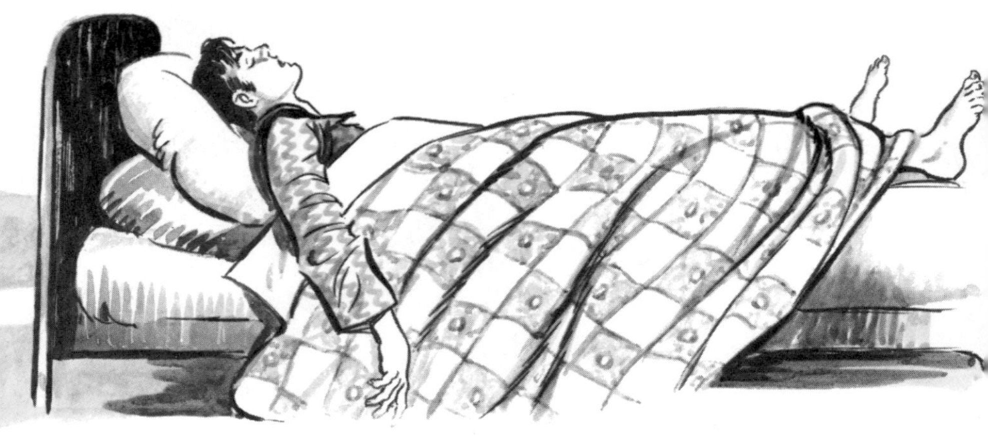

But last night his father had warned him.

"If Bruff doesn't do as he's told," his father had said, "he goes!"

Jerry put on his shoes.

Rod snored again. He was lying on his back. His feet stuck out of the bottom of his bed.

"Rod! Wake up!" Jerry called into Rod's ear.

Rod slept on. Jerry had plans for Rod.

"It's eight o'clock!" Jerry called.

He pulled the bed-clothes off Rod. Then he darted from the room.

Jerry crept down the stairs. Silently he opened the front door. Then, still silently, he crept to the garage.

He opened the garage door. His father's car nearly filled the garage. But at the other end of the garage was a big box. In the box was an old rug and an old blanket. It was the bed that Jerry had made yesterday.

Sitting up in the bed was Bruff.

"Bruff!" called Jerry.

The boxer bounded out of the bed. His stump of a tail wagged. In three bounds Bruff came to Jerry. The dog's brown eyes lit up. He leapt up and pushed his cold, wet nose into Jerry's face.

Jerry slipped the lead over Bruff's head.

"Come on, Bruff," said Jerry. "You must be hungry!"

He picked up the dog's bowl. Then, with Bruff wagging himself along at his side, he went back to the house.

In the kitchen, Jerry filled Bruff's bowl. He had to use all the food that was left.

Jerry put the bowl down on the kitchen floor. Bruff began eating hungrily.

"I must get some meat and some bones to-day," Jerry thought.

As Bruff ate hungrily, Jerry was grinning. Yesterday morning he hadn't had a dog. Now he had Bruff. Yesterday morning seemed as far away as life on another planet.

Yesterday afternoon Jerry had read in the newspaper that someone was trying to find a good home for a boxer dog. Straight away, Jerry had made his plan to get that boxer.

Jerry was always making plans. But this plan had worked. He had got Rod to help him. Jerry grinned to himself as he thought of it. Rod's friend, Jill Wells, had brought her puppy, a boxer called Goldie, to show to his mother.

As soon as Mrs. Raven had said that she wished she had a puppy like Goldie, Jerry had told her that he could get her one.

From then on things had moved fast. Jerry had made them move fast! Before his mother or father knew what was happening, Jerry had got them to agree to give the boxer a good home.

Jerry and his father had gone in the car to get Bruff. The little old lady who owned Bruff lived in a narrow house in a narrow street. Bruff was too big and too lively for her to control. Jerry was quite sure he could control Bruff.

But as soon as they were home with Bruff, Jerry's father began to think he had been wrong to let Jerry have the dog.

Now Bruff was here, in the kitchen, licking his bowl clean. Jerry watched his dog proudly. The old lady, who had owned Bruff, had given Jerry the dog's bowl and some food. She had also given him a buff envelope. Inside the envelope Jerry had found Bruff's pedigree.

When Jerry read Bruff's pedigree he knew why Bruff looked such a fine dog. Bruff came from a long line of champions. Jerry knew that whatever happened, he must keep Bruff.

But that was just the trouble. Jerry knew that Bruff was still untrained. Bruff was a fine dog. He was strong and quick. But about the only thing Bruff knew was his name. Somehow or other, Jerry had to train him. If Bruff didn't do as he was told, then his father would say he had to go.

"Come on, Bruff!" said Jerry. "Let's get Rod out of bed!"

Silently, Jerry and Bruff went upstairs. Once in his bedroom, Jerry shut the door.

Rod was lying on his back. The bed-clothes were on the floor. Rod was still fast asleep.

"Where's Rod?" said Jerry.

At once Bruff took one bound and landed on top of Rod. Jerry was pleased. Already Bruff knew who Rod was!

The boxer's cold, wet face was all over Rod's face.

"Get Bruff off!" cried Rod. He was wide awake now. He was not pleased!

"Down, Bruff!" said Jerry, pulling Bruff off Rod.

"He's a good alarm-clock!" Jerry said to his brother, grinning. "He wakes you up and gives you a wash at the same time!"

"What's the time?" demanded Rod.

"Ten past six," Jerry told him. "Get up, Rod. We've got to get the wire-netting."

"What wire-netting?" asked Rod, sleepily.

"You said you'd get the wire-netting to put on top of the fence so that Bruff can't get out of the garden," said Jerry.

"Did I?" asked Rod with a smile. "I'm meeting Jill Wells at nine o'clock."

"But you said you'd get the wire and help me!" Jerry said in alarm. "Jill Wells!"

"You were glad of Jill's help yesterday with Goldie," Rod told him. Then he grinned. "To-day we're going into town. Her father's taking us in his car."

"You said you'd help me," Jerry said again. "If Bruff gets out of the garden and gets into trouble, Dad will say he's got to go!"

"I know," said Rod. He pulled the bed-clothes over himself and shut his eyes. "Call me at half-past seven, Jerry, and take that dog away."

"No!" snapped Jerry.

"I should if I were you," said Rod.

"Why?" demanded Jerry. "You get yourself up."

"All right, then," said Rod, grinning now. "But if I don't meet Jill at nine then you won't get your wire!"

"What do you mean?" asked Jerry.

"We're going to town to get the wire," said his brother. "We'll bring it back in the car."

"Thanks, Rod," said Jerry. "But you'd better get up now."

"Why?" asked Rod.

"Because we've got to find some posts and dig holes for them," Jerry told him. "Then when you bring the wire-netting we'll be ready to put it up."

"I wish you'd stop making plans!" laughed Rod.

"Where's Rod!" said Jerry to Bruff.

"All right," said Rod. "I'll get up!"

Rod knew it was no good. Jerry wouldn't let him sleep. The sooner Jerry got the fence fixed so that Bruff couldn't get out, the better. Rod got out of bed. He knew, too, that if he didn't, Bruff would be on top of him giving him another wash.

"While you're getting dressed," said Jerry, "I'll take Bruff for a run. It will help to make him quiet when Mum and Dad get up."

"Mind Bruff doesn't take *you* for a run!" said Rod.

DOG GONE!

When Mr. and Mrs. Raven got up they found Jerry and Rod hard at work in the garden.

"What's going on?" demanded Mr. Raven, as they sat eating breakfast.

"We've been putting up posts for the wire-netting," Jerry said. "It's to stop Bruff getting out."

"Who said you could use those bean-sticks?" asked his father.

"I thought you wouldn't mind, Dad," said Rod. "I'm paying for the wire-netting myself."

"It's only until I get Bruff trained," added Jerry.

"I see," said their father. "Well, mind you do train him. I don't want that dog making a mess of my garden."

Mr. Raven got up. It was time he left for work. It was going to be another hot day driving his crane.

"It's time I was going," said Mr. Raven. He turned to Jerry. "Make sure you keep that dog of yours out of trouble, Jerry."

"Yes, Dad," said Jerry. "Bruff will be all right."

His father went off to work. Jerry waited until his mother came back into the room after seeing his father off.

"Mum, I'll have to get some food for Bruff to-day," he said.

"What will Bruff eat?" asked his mother.

"Oh, just meat, biscuits and bones," said Jerry. "I'll need some money, Mum."

"How much meat will you want?" asked his mother.

"Well," said Jerry, "Bruff needs a kilo a day."

"A kilo of meat!" exclaimed Mrs. Raven. "That's more meat than we eat!"

"Oh, Bruff won't eat best English beef!" Jerry said. "Just scraps. I'll see what the butcher has."

"It's a good job your father didn't know that Bruff will need a kilo of meat every day!" said Mrs. Raven. "He'd have had a fit! You didn't say anything about this yesterday, Jerry."

"I didn't want to give you a shock, Mum," said Jerry, with a smile. "But a ten months old boxer needs three meals a day," he added.

"Three meals a day!" exclaimed Mrs. Raven.

"There's one thing about Jerry," said his brother Rod, "he's always giving us shocks. But he only gives them to us one at a time!"

Mrs. Raven shook her head. She didn't think Jerry would keep Bruff for long. His father would not put up with the dog making trouble. She hoped Bruff wouldn't stay long. Cooking for Jerry and Rod and their father was hard work. Now she had to cook for a dog as well!

After breakfast Jerry and Rod finished putting up the bean-sticks for the wire-netting. Then Rod went off with Jill Wells in her father's car.

Jerry gave Bruff a good brushing. Bruff's coat shone like cloth of gold. The white marks on his face and chest were like snow.

"I'm going to see the butcher, Mum," said Jerry. "Can I have some money, please?"

Once Jerry had the money he was off. He tried to make Bruff walk at his heels. But Bruff pulled ahead. Jerry knew he had a lot of training to do before Bruff would walk to heel.

When Jerry got back home he was carrying a large parcel wrapped in newspaper.

"Cheer up, Mum!" Jerry called as he marched into the kitchen. His face wore a large grin.

"The butcher says Bruff is such a fine boxer that I can have all the scraps and bones I want," Jerry told his mother. "For nothing! Free!"

"That's good news," his mother said, smiling. "And what did you tell the butcher?" she asked.

"Er, well, er," began Jerry, "well, Mum, I told him that we'd had to give Bruff a good home. Then I showed him Bruff's pedigree. I said, well, Mum, I told him that I wanted to make Bruff a champion and put him in dog shows."

"I thought you must have told the butcher a fine old tale. Butchers don't give meat away!" said Mrs. Raven.

Jerry gave Bruff a large bone. The boxer lay on the grass, the bone between his paws, and chewed away happily.

As soon as Rod came back with the wire-netting, the two brothers set to work. They used some old wire to tie the wire-netting to the bean-sticks.

The garden fence was just about a metre high. Bruff could jump it easily. But now, with the wire-netting on top of the fence, Bruff would have to jump much higher.

Jerry and Rod had just finished tying the wire-netting down to the old fence when their mother called them to dinner.

"Thanks, Rod," said Jerry. "Bruff can't get over that. And there aren't any gaps between the fence and the netting. He'll not get out now."

They left Bruff, still chewing happily at his bone on the grass, and went in to dinner. Jerry sat down and looked hungrily at his plate.

"You haven't fed Bruff yet," his mother told him. "He needs three meals a day. You said so yourself. That bone's not a meal!"

Jerry grinned. His mother was right. When it came to food, his mother was always right! He got up to get Bruff's bowl. When he found it, it was already full.

"Thanks, Mum," he called. "I could almost eat this myself!"

He took the bowl out to Bruff. The boxer bounded to him. He put the bowl down and Bruff nose-dived into the food.

Jerry went to eat his own dinner. He was ready for it.

"Bruff will need a sleep after all that food," he told his mother. "But I bet that bowl's empty—Bruff's a hungry dog!"

As soon as Jerry and Rod had finished their meal they went out into the garden. Bruff's bowl was empty.

The garden was empty, too.

"Bruff's gone!" yelled Jerry.

Jerry raced round the garden trying to find where the dog had got out.

"Here! Look at this!" called Rod.

Jerry ran to where Rod was standing by the side gate. The side gate, between the Raven's house and the house next door, was too high for Bruff to jump.

"Look," said Rod. He pointed to the bottom of the gate.

There was a large gap under the gate.

"We forgot about that," said Rod.

"I'll go and find Bruff," Jerry said. "He could be anywhere." He wondered if he would ever find his boxer again.

"I'll block this gap up," Rod told him.

Rod knew how Jerry must feel. He had only had his dog a day. Already the dog had gone.

Jerry opened the side gate and ran out into the street.

"Bruff!" he called.

But there was no sign of Bruff.

THE CHASE

Jerry raced down the street. As he ran he looked into gardens. He looked down each side road that he crossed. Soon he was wet through with sweat.

He ran on. He knew that there were no houses after the next corner. After that there was nothing but fields.

Jerry swung round the corner. As he did so, he saw Bruff.

The boxer was a long way off. Jerry saw Bruff go through a gap in the hedge.

As fast as he could, Jerry raced after Bruff. As he burst through the gap in the hedge, his heart sank.

In the field was a herd of cows. Round the herd of cows raced Bruff.

"Bruff!" Jerry called.

But Jerry knew it was no good. All the time Bruff was closing in, getting nearer and nearer to the cows. Jerry thought of stories he had read of bulldogs and boxers fighting bulls.

Jerry ran after the dog. Some of the cows were watching Bruff. One cow lowered its head as the boxer raced towards it.

As Bruff skidded past the cow, the cow drove its horns at him. Bruff, only a pace away, raced on.

Suddenly, Jerry knew that he would never catch Bruff. Not only was Bruff too fast for him, Bruff didn't see him or hear him.

Then one of the cows, its head down, left the herd. Slowly it began following Bruff. Then it broke into a trot.

Bruff bounded past Jerry without seeing him. Something about the look on Bruff's face told Jerry that Bruff was happy. He almost seemed to be grinning.

Jerry knew now that Bruff was just having fun. He was in a field full of animal smells. There were animals moving about. Jerry understood now. Bruff wasn't chasing the cows. He didn't want to fight them. For Bruff this was just a game.

But Jerry could also see that the cows didn't think this was just fun and games. To the cows, this was trouble. A wild dog was chasing them.

The cow which had left the herd was moving faster now. Bruff swung round in front of the cow. As he did so the cow's horns jabbed forward. To Jerry it looked as if the horns hit Bruff in the ribs. But the boxer zig-zagged away.

Now Bruff was racing at full speed straight down the field towards Jerry. At once, Jerry knew what to do. Instead of chasing Bruff, he ran away from him.

"Bruff!" he called, as he ran. "Bruff!"

Jerry did not run fast, letting the dog get near to him. Looking over his shoulder, he saw the boxer pounding after him. All the time Bruff was getting nearer.

This was a game Bruff understood. He was chasing Jerry now. Jerry made for the far side of the field. He kept well away from the cows.

With Bruff panting hard behind him, Jerry shot through the gap in the hedge.

A big hand grabbed Jerry's arm.

"Where do you think you're going?" a gruff voice demanded.

Jerry looked up into the angry face of the farmer.

"I've been watching you," the farmer went on. "You and this mad dog of yours! You were chasing my cows!"

"No," panted Jerry. "My dog got out. I came to get him. He's only a puppy. He . . ."

"Don't lie to me!" shouted the farmer. His face was red with anger. He still held Jerry's arm. "I saw you!"

Out of the corner of his eye, Jerry saw Bruff. Bruff's eyes were on the farmer. He was about to spring at the man.

"Look out!" cried Jerry. "He'll go for you!"

Not a moment too soon, the farmer let go of Jerry's arm.

Bruff came and stood between Jerry and the farmer. The boxer's head was up, his lower jaw was pushed forward. His eyes stared at the man.

"Look at him! He'd go for me!" exclaimed the farmer. "A puppy, indeed! What's your name and address?"

Jerry told him.

"You're on my land. That animal's got no collar and he's not on a lead. He's wild—out of control!" said the farmer. He stared at Bruff. Bruff stared back at him. "Now get off my land! Go on, the pair of you! And don't let me see you again. If that dog chases my cows again—I'll shoot it! Go on—that way!"

The farmer pointed to a footpath. Jerry knew it led down to the river. It would be a long way home. He took hold of Bruff's neck.

Jerry was angry now. But he knew that Bruff shouldn't have been in the field with the cows.

"Sorry," Jerry said to the farmer.

"Off you go!" shouted the farmer. "And keep away from my cows! If he gets after them again, I'll shoot him!"

Jerry knew that he would.

He held on to Bruff's neck until they came to the footpath. Then he let Bruff go. The boxer ran ahead and waited for him. Jerry walked along the path. Sweat ran down his face. His shirt stuck to him. Slowly, his anger went. He had found Bruff.

Perhaps it would be cool by the river.

BRUFF BY THE RIVER

With Bruff beside him, Jerry Raven stopped at the gate. He looked over the gate into the next field. He made sure that there were no cows, bulls, pigs or hens about.

Jerry climbed over the gate. Bruff leapt over after him.

Jerry was thinking hard. Bruff was smart but he was full of fun. He wasn't wild but he did wild things. He knew his name but, if you called him, he only came if he wanted to come. He was brave, too.

"It's going to be a hard job training him," Jerry said to himself. "And it's going to be an even harder job keeping him out of trouble!"

He threw some sticks for Bruff. The boxer chased after them. Sometimes he caught the stick in the air. Jerry tried to get him to bring the stick back to him. But that was something else Bruff still had to learn.

When they came to the path which ran along the bank of the river Bruff shot ahead. Jerry broke into a trot after him. Then he saw that Bruff was racing after a young woman.

"Bruff!" Jerry called.

The young woman was wearing a light yellow dress. The dress flashed in the sunlight. She was walking slowly, her back to Jerry and to Bruff.

"Look out!" called Jerry.

But the young woman strolled slowly on. Bruff was racing nearer and nearer. Then he reared up and his two forepaws came down on the woman's shoulders.

Jerry saw her turn. She stared into Bruff's face. Then she let out a yell and fled.

As she ran, one of her shoes came off. Bruff trotted lightly after her and picked up the shoe. Then, with the shoe between his teeth, he raced back to Jerry.

Jerry threw himself upon the dog and got the shoe from his mouth. He kept a firm hold of Bruff.

"He's all right!" Jerry called to the young woman. "He won't hurt. He's only a puppy."

At last the woman stopped running. With one shoe on and one shoe off she couldn't have run any further if she had wanted to.

Jerry caught up with her.

"I'm sorry," said Jerry, not for the first or last time that day. "He's only playing." He gave the woman her shoe.

"Oh dear," she panted. "It was such a shock. He's so big! I nearly jumped in the river."

"Sorry, Miss," Jerry said again.

Bruff, with Jerry still holding him, was now licking her hand. Jerry told her how Bruff had got out of the garden.

"You're a bad dog," she said, smiling at Bruff. "But I'll let you off this time!"

"Thanks, Miss," said Jerry. He gave the young woman a winning smile. "You're a sport!"

Then Jerry and Bruff ran off. Jerry only wished he could find some rope for a lead. He was beginning to think that he would never get Bruff home. He tried to keep a grip on the dog's neck.

But Bruff had suddenly smelt food. He gave a quick twist and was free from Jerry's grip. Then he was off, following his nose to the food.

Too late, Jerry saw where Bruff was going.

A little way from the river bank was a tree. Under the tree were a man and a woman. Between them, on the grass, was a white tablecloth. On the tablecloth was set out a picnic meal. Bruff just helped himself!

As Bruff's teeth closed on a slice of ham, the man made a grab at him.

Now boxers, when they are eating, do not like to be grabbed. Bruff let out a growl. The woman grabbed what was left of the picnic. Bruff made a grab at the ham. He missed and got the white tablecloth. The man tried to get the tablecloth. Bruff raced away.

With the tablecloth streaming out behind him, Bruff ran back to Jerry. Jerry just got a grip on the tablecloth as it streamed past him. Then Bruff was at one end of the cloth and Jerry was at the other.

Bruff pulled. Jerry pulled. This game was just to Bruff's liking. He spread out his legs and pulled. Jerry was sure that at any moment the cloth would tear.

Quickly Jerry went hand over hand up the cloth until he got to Bruff's teeth. Then he put one hand over the dog's nose and got his fingers in on both sides of his upper jaw. The tablecloth came away, still in one piece.

"That dog's not safe!" said the man. "He should be on a lead."

"I know," Jerry agreed. "I'm sorry."

He gave the tablecloth back to the woman.

"You'd better take him away," said the woman. "He's already eaten our ham."

"Sorry," said Jerry again.

Back by the river, Jerry suddenly felt old. He felt as old as his father.

It was as if he had changed places with his father and Bruff had changed places with Jerry.

"You're just like me," Jerry said to Bruff. "You're always running head-first into trouble!"

But, Jerry knew, it wasn't just as simple as that. There was still his father. Bruff's troubles were Jerry's troubles. And his father didn't like trouble.

Without thinking what he was doing, Jerry picked up a stick and threw it into the river.

Bruff dived down the bank head-first after the stick. He hit the water with a splash and began swimming.

Jerry forgot all about trouble.

Bruff was swimming fast down-stream.

"Go on, Bruff!" called Jerry. "Swim for it!"

He was delighted to see Bruff take to the water like a duck. He began running along the bank. Bruff had been hot after racing about. He had never swum before and now the cool water was good. He swam on, his head and shoulders out of the water, and soon found that he could swim wherever he wanted to go.

On the bank Bruff saw some boys and girls sunbathing. He swam to the bank and leapt out. But being wet in the water was one thing. Being wet out of the water was another. Bruff shook himself.

Yells, shouts and laughs went up from the children as Bruff sent water splashing over them. The children jumped up and grabbed their towels.

Bruff, delighted by this game, grabbed a mouthful of clothes. He ran off. The children chased after him.

Jerry was laughing helplessly. He was laughing helplessly because Bruff had got out of the river on the other bank. So now Jerry was on one side of the river and there was Bruff, being chased by the children, on the other.

The girls and boys at last drove Bruff back towards the river.

"Corner him!" called a boy.

"Get him!" called a girl.

A boy threw himself at Bruff. Bruff turned. He dived into the river.

Then, as he swam, he let go of the clothes in his mouth. Soon Bruff was heading down-stream with a fleet of socks, shirts and vests behind him.

Hooting with laughter, the girls and boys dived in after their clothes.

"Bruff!" Jerry called.

Bruff turned in mid-stream and made for the bank. He leapt out as Jerry ran up to him. This time Jerry had some rope which he had found on the bank. He put it round Bruff's neck.

Bruff shook himself dry all over Jerry.

A hoot of laughter went up from the children on the other bank.

DOG FIGHT

Jerry made up for lost time now. With Bruff kept firmly to heel he ran along the path by the river.

"Hi, Jerry!" Jerry heard his brother call.

Near the bridge Rod and Jill Wells were walking towards him. Jill had Goldie, her boxer puppy, with her.

Once Bruff saw Goldie he pulled ahead, dragging Jerry after him.

"I thought we'd lost you and the dog," joked Rod.

"He's a smashing boxer," said Jill.

"Smashing's the word for it," laughed Jerry, thinking of his father.

Bruff put his head down to the puppy. The puppy put up a paw. Bruff boxed back.

"Look at them!" exclaimed Jill. "Look how good Bruff is with Goldie."

Bruff and Goldie boxed playfully, while Jill, Rod and Jerry watched them. Suddenly a barking, black dog landed between Goldie and Bruff.

"Blackie!" warned Jerry, as Jill picked up her puppy.

The black dog snapped at Goldie. Rod knocked Blackie back as it jumped up snapping at Goldie. Then it turned and faced Bruff. Jerry saw its angry, snarling face. Barking and snapping, it came towards Bruff.

Jerry felt the rope burn his hand as Bruff leapt forward and tore himself free. Then Bruff was on top of the dog, knocking it sideways to the ground. Jerry saw Blackie's teeth snap shut only an inch from Bruff's neck. Bruff jumped clear and waited for Blackie to turn and face him. Bruff's teeth flashed white from his black mask.

Now Blackie, the fur standing out like a ruff round its neck, barked wildly and then leapt at Bruff. Again Blackie's teeth struck at Bruff's neck. But Bruff, light as a cat, jumped clear into the air. Blackie landed and Bruff fell on him. Bruff's jaws closed on Blackie's neck, pinning the dog to the ground.

Blackie let out a howl. Bruff suddenly threw the dog in the air. Its legs struck out as it tried to turn in the air. Then its back hit the ground. It let out another howl. Bruff dived at Blackie again.

But Blackie had had enough. Its tail down, it fled. Bruff gave his first gruff growl. Then he chased after the dog until he was sure it would not turn again. The fight was over. Bruff ran back to Jerry.

Jerry patted and fussed Bruff's head.

Jill put Goldie down again.

"It's a good job Bruff was here," said Jill. "That Blackie is always barking and fighting."

"I don't like dog fights," said Rod. "But Bruff knows how to look after himself. Blackie won't want to fight Bruff again!"

"I'd better go," said Jerry. He didn't want Rod to ask him what had happened that afternoon. "Cheerio, Jill."

Jerry and Bruff went off towards the bridge. They went up the path to the road. From there, with Bruff tugging on the rope, they were home in ten minutes.

Jerry had had enough, too, for one afternoon.

He put on Bruff's lead. Jerry made up his mind never to go looking for Bruff without a lead again. He tied the lead to some rope so that the dog could wander about the garden. Then he gave Bruff a bowl of water. Bruff lapped up the water. Then he lay down in the shade of the house.

"Enough is enough!" said Jerry to himself. "Even for Bruff!"

TROUBLE!

"Can I go for a swim, Mum?" Jerry asked.

"Will Bruff be all right? I've got to do some shopping," said his mother, "so I can't keep an eye on him."

"Oh, he's asleep," Jerry told her, "and I've tied him up and left a bone for him. I wanted to start training him but I'll have to do that this evening."

"All right," his mother agreed, "but get back in time for tea when your father comes home."

"O.K.," called Jerry.

He checked that Bruff was still sleeping and went off for his swim.

The river was full of the bobbing heads of boys and girls Jerry knew. But Jerry went to a spot where he could be on his own. He wanted to think.

He dived in and the cold water hit him. He felt better at once. He turned over on his back and kicked out with his legs. Looking up he could see the blue sky between the dark green of the trees. In mid-stream he settled into a strong crawl that drove him up-stream. Jerry swam well and when he swam he thought only about swimming.

Now the water felt warm. Jerry swam back and got out onto the bank. He gave his tanned body and mop of hair a quick rub. Then he stretched out on his towel. He began to think about Bruff.

Rod and Jill found Jerry fast asleep. Goldie woke him up by putting his cold nose in Jerry's ear.

"Bruff," said Jerry, waking with a start. He sat up.

"Catching up on your sleep?" asked Rod.

"Oh no," grinned Jerry. "I'd just shut my eyes to keep the sun out."

"It's half-past five," Rod told him. "We'll go on. It's time we got back for tea."

"I'll catch you up," said Jerry, jumping up.

Jill and Rod, with Goldie trotting at the end of his lead, walked away along the bank. Jerry threw himself into his clothes. Then he ran home, taking a short cut, to make sure he was home before Rod.

As Jerry ran round the side of the house his father was waiting for him.

"Come and look at this," said his father.

Jerry knew his father wasn't going to show him anything he would want to see.

"Look!" said his father. He pointed to where the row of runner-beans had stood. Now the bean sticks and the beans were down on the ground.

"And look at that!" said his father.

Jerry looked. In the middle of a row of potatoes was a hole as deep and as wide as a dog. At the bottom of the hole was a bone. The earth from the hole covered half of the strawberry bed.

"That's not all! Look at the flowers!" his father exclaimed.

In one of the borders a few flowers still waved their heads. But most of the flowers had lost their heads. The blooms had been bitten off.

"Sorry, Dad," Jerry said. "It was . . ."

"I know it was that dog," his father snapped. "You go off swimming and forget all about the dog!"

"He was asleep, Dad," said Jerry. "I tied him up. I didn't want him to be just on his lead so I tied his lead to some rope. He must have got it round the beans. That's how . . ."

"And where's Roderick? He's just as bad! He goes off with that Jill of his and her dog!" his father said.

"Rod helped me put up the fence all morning and . . ." began Jerry.

"Fine," replied his father, "just to make sure that that dog can stay in my garden and pull it to bits! I don't . . ."

"Tom!" Mrs. Raven called her husband. "Tom, there's someone to see you."

Red in the face, Mr. Raven marched into the house.

Quickly Jerry set to work. He got the bone out of the hole and filled it in, taking care to get the earth off the strawberry bed as best he could.

All this time Bruff had been pulling on his lead trying to get to Jerry. But Jerry worked on. He hoped that whoever had come to see his father would keep him talking a long time.

Jerry began to put up some of the bean-sticks.

"Jerry!" called his father from the house. "Come here!"

Jerry knew he was not being called to have his tea.

"Do you know who that was?" his father asked.

"No, Dad," Jerry answered.

"The farmer from Cross Farm!" his father shouted. "Do you know why?"

"Yes, Dad," Jerry replied. His face fell.

"Because that dog of yours has been chasing his cows!"

"Well, Dad . . ."

"And you were chasing them, too! What about it, eh?" demanded his father.

"Bruff wasn't chasing them," said Jerry. "He was just running round the field. He's never seen cows before and . . ."

"And what's this about the dog going for the farmer? Do you know what he said? He said that if the dog gets on his farm again he'll shoot it. He said it was running wild—out of control!" Mr. Raven glared at his son. "Train the dog, indeed! You can't train yourself!"

"Tea's ready!" called Mrs. Raven.

"If that dog does one more thing wrong—then it goes," warned Mr. Raven. "One more thing and I'll ring up the Animal Rescue people and they can take him away! Do you understand?"

"Yes, Dad," Jerry said sadly.

Tea began without a word being spoken. Jerry just ate. Then Rod came in.

"That Bruff's a lot of dog!" began Rod.

No one spoke. Rod thought everyone wanted him to go on.

"Didn't Jerry tell you? Bruff took to the water as if he'd been swimming all his life. Some of the lads were telling me about him. I wish I'd been there. I'd have given anything to have seen him dive in with his mouth full of clothes!" Rod was laughing.

"What's that?" demanded his father. He wasn't laughing. He looked at Jerry.

Jerry told him what had happened.

"And then I met Mary Cliff," Rod went on. "She said she nearly jumped in the river when Bruff jumped on her back! She ran so hard her shoe came off!"

Jerry kicked him under the table. But Rod went on.

"Did Jerry tell you about the fight?" he asked. "That Blackie won't forget it. Bruff was on to him in a flash. Threw him in the air and . . ."

"That's enough! That's all I want to hear!" their father said. "That dog's been running wild all day. Chasing cows, chasing young women, chasing dogs, pulling my garden to bits! And you think it's all a joke! Well, I don't. I've already told Jerry that if that dog does one more thing wrong, then I'll get rid of it!"

"Bruff's not trained, that's all, Dad," said Jerry.

"He's just full of fun," added Rod.

"You two have got a funny way of having fun, that's all I can say," replied their father.

"We've only had Bruff a day," said their mother. "And look at the trouble he's caused. What's he going to do next, I wonder?"

"The next time will be the last time," said their father. He got up from the table and went into the garden.

Bruff got up and wagged his tail at him.

Mr. Raven walked straight by Bruff without looking at him.

"I'll train him, Mum," said Jerry. "I know what to do. I've been reading books about training dogs."

"I've been reading books about motor-bikes for years," said Rod with a smile. "But I've never ridden one. I only hope you know how to train Bruff, Jerry."

"I'm going to start now," Jerry said. "You can help me, Rod. Come on."

Jerry and Rod went out into the garden.

Jerry knew just what to do.

Did Bruff?

HOW TO TRAIN BOYS

"The first thing," Jerry told his brother, "is to get Bruff to come when he's called."

"What do we do?" Rod asked.

"You take him to the other end of the grass," said Jerry. "When I call him you let him go."

Rod took Bruff and held him.

"Bruff!" called Jerry.

The dog trotted to Jerry. Jerry held him, patting him and making a fuss of him.

"Now you call him," said Jerry.

"Bruff!" called Rod.

This time the dog trotted to Rod. Rod patted him and fussed him until Jerry again called Bruff.

They did this a dozen times each.

"Once more," said Jerry. "Bruff!" he called.

Bruff trotted towards Jerry. Then he sat down on the grass. He began licking his white chest.

"Don't call him," warned Jerry. "Just hold him until I get back."

Jerry went into the house and came back with two bags filled with bits of meat. He gave one bag to Rod. Bruff tried to jump up as soon as he smelt the meat.

"Bruff!" called Jerry.

This time Bruff bounded to Jerry. Jerry gave him a small bit of meat.

"Go to the bottom of the garden," Jerry told Rod. "Then call him."

"Bruff!" called Rod, from the bottom of the garden.

In a great rush, Bruff shot down the garden. He bounded past Mr. Raven who did not look up. He was putting up the bean sticks. Bruff went up to Rod, his tail wagging. Rod gave him some meat.

"Hold him till I've hidden in the house," called Jerry. "When he comes to me, you hide in the garden, Rod. Then call him."

Jerry ran into the living-room and hid behind an armchair. Then he called Bruff.

Bruff came straight to him.

"Good boy!" exclaimed Jerry. The training was going well.

"Bruff!" called Rod.

Bruff raced out of the house and went straight to Rod who had hidden behind a bush.

Jerry and Rod kept Bruff on the move, running backwards and forwards to them when they called, for another five minutes.

"Now take him into the front garden, Rod. I'll stay here," said Jerry.

Rod took Bruff into the small front garden. He held Bruff until Jerry called.

"Bruff!" called Jerry.

Bruff raced away. He shot into the street.

"Jerry! Quick!" called Rod.

Jerry knew what had happened. He ran to the front garden.

"Which way did he go?" Jerry asked.

"There he is," said Rod, pointing down the street to the left. Bruff was sitting by a wall. On top of the wall was a grey cat.

Jerry called Bruff, but the dog had eyes and ears only for the cat. He leapt up, but the wall was too high. The cat did not move.

Again Bruff leapt. This time the grey cat's paw struck Bruff across the nose. Jerry heard Bruff howl. The cat jumped down on the other side of the wall.

"Bruff!" Jerry called.

This time Bruff came to Jerry. His stump of a tail was down.

"Hit him," said Rod, "for not coming when you called him the first time!"

"No," Jerry told his brother. "If I hit him he won't want to come to me when I call him!" He gave Bruff the last bit of meat. "I want him to *want* to come. But that cat did a good job for us!"

"Perhaps we should get a cat to train him!" said Rod with a laugh.

They went back to the garden.

"I want to train him to walk to heel," Jerry said.

"How do you do that?" asked Rod.

"You put on his lead like this," said Jerry, showing his brother. He put the lead over Bruff's head. "Now, if he pulls, the loop goes tight round his neck."

Then Jerry stood and faced the same way as Bruff. The dog was on his left and he held the end of the lead in his right hand. His left hand was free.

"If I pull up with my right hand the loop goes tight," Jerry explained. As he spoke, Bruff pulled ahead. The lead went tight and Bruff stopped.

"Doesn't it hurt him?" asked Rod.

"No," Jerry said with a smile. "Bruff's neck is too strong. But it tells him to stop pulling!"

"Is that all you have to do?" demanded Rod. "It doesn't seem to make Bruff keep to heel," he added as Bruff pulled ahead.

"That's because Bruff wasn't trained when he was a puppy," said Jerry. "That's the trouble with Bruff! He wasn't trained when he was young."

"That's what Dad says is the trouble with you!" joked Rod.

"I'm not a dog," laughed Jerry.

He began walking round the grass with Bruff on the slip lead. Soon Bruff began to keep just behind Jerry's left leg.

From time to time Jerry turned quickly to the left. Bruff bumped into his leg. Sometimes Jerry turned right round. It made the boxer keep back.

"Good boy," said Jerry, when Bruff was well to heel. With his left hand he patted the dog's head.

"Let me have a go," said Rod.

Rod now took the lead and led Bruff round and round the grass. He found that it was hard work. But, little by little, Bruff stopped pulling ahead and kept to heel.

"You'll wear that grass out if you go on like that," called their father.

"We'll take him for a walk," Jerry called back.

They took Bruff down by the river. As soon as they left the house, Bruff wanted to pull ahead. Rod's arm hurt from holding Bruff back.

Jerry took over. At last Bruff seemed to settle down. He stopped pulling. He no longer tried to sniff every tree they passed. He didn't try to pull ahead when they got near to people.

"He walks well," said Rod. "He lifts his feet up well."

"That's how a boxer should walk," Jerry agreed, proudly.

"Shall we let him off his lead?" said Rod.

"No," said Jerry. He shook his head knowingly. "He'd be off like a shot. I want to take him home without any more trouble!"

"Do you think you can keep him out of trouble, Jerry?" Rod asked.

"No!" Jerry answered, as quick as a flash.

"What about Dad? You know what he said," said Rod.

It was dusk now. A small wind played on the river. Jerry walked on, Bruff by his side. He was thinking. Then he said:

"I don't know. Bruff's a good dog. I don't want Dad to get rid of him. But Bruff's like me. He just jumps into trouble—with all four feet!"

"Dad's had enough of him," said Rod. "I'll do all I can to help you, Jerry. But, if Bruff does anything wrong, I'm sure Dad will say he has to go."

"Thanks," said Jerry. "I'll pay you back for the wire-netting. I know you want that motor-bike."

"Forget it," Rod told his brother. "And the motor-bike's off!"

"Off!" exclaimed Jerry. "Why?"

"It's Jill," Rod said. "She wants a car or nothing now!"

"A car! I thought she wanted you to get a motor-bike," said Jerry.

"She says she can't take Goldie on a motor-bike," Rod explained.

"Girls!" laughed Jerry.

TROUBLE AT NIGHT

Jerry and Rod got back home feeling tired. They both felt older, too.

"It's your bed-time," said his father to Jerry.

"I'll just put Bruff to bed in the garage," Jerry replied.

"Look sharp about it," said his father.

Jerry did. He got a bone and some food for Bruff. Then he took him to the garage.

"Bed!" he said.

Bruff went straight to his box. Jerry put the food down beside him. Then he stroked and patted Bruff. Suddenly Jerry felt this might be the last time. Bruff rolled over. His white feet boxed. On his face was a happy grin.

"It's up to you, Bruff, if you want to stay," said Jerry.

He gave Bruff a last pat. Then he went out of the garage. He had a drink of milk in the kitchen and ate a biscuit.

"Good-night!" he called.

He went up to bed and fell asleep thinking of how he could keep Bruff out of trouble.

Downstairs Mr. Raven put down his newspaper.

"I've just spent the evening putting the garden straight," he said to Rod.

"Yes, Dad," Rod agreed. "You know, Dad, Jerry's doing his best with Bruff. I'm sure he'll train the dog. We've got to give him time to . . ."

"Time!" his father exclaimed. "He's only had the dog twenty-four hours and look what it's got up to!"

"But Rod's right," put in Mrs. Raven. "Jerry and Rod worked all morning. . . ."

"And I worked all evening!" added Mr. Raven.

"They worked all morning putting that netting up," Mrs. Raven went on. "Rod spent his own money. Jerry was having his dinner when the dog got out of the garden. I know the farmer says that the dog was chasing his cows. But Jerry was there and he got the dog away."

"That's right, Dad," added Rod.

"I see," said Mr. Raven. He wasn't angry any more. He spoke quietly. "I see," he said again. "So I'm the one that's wrong."

"Well, dear," Mrs. Raven said quietly, "you took Jerry to get the dog. You let him have it. If you ask me . . ."

"Yes, dear," Mr. Raven agreed. "I was wrong. I was wrong."

Rod thought things were going well. He picked up the paper. He wanted to see if there were any cars for sale. Maybe there was a Car Rescue Centre! Perhaps someone had a Rolls Royce that wanted a good home!

"And if I was wrong," Mr. Raven suddenly said, "I'm the one to put things right! If that dog causes any more trouble I'm getting rid of it. So you'd better make sure, Roderick, that it *keeps* out of trouble."

"Yes, Dad," Roderick said from behind the newspaper.

"What was that?" asked his mother.

"What, dear?" asked his father.

"I thought I heard something," his mother answered.

"It sounds like Jerry snoring," said Rod. He had heard the sound. It had sounded like Bruff.

Rod thought quickly.

"Can I have the television on to see the cricket scores?" he asked.

He knew that the sports news wouldn't be on. But he hoped that the sound of the television would stop his father from hearing Bruff.

"No, listen a minute," his father said.

"It's Bruff!" said his mother.

The sound of barking came from the garage.

"At this time of night!" said his father.

"Oh dear," said his mother, "we don't want Bruff to wake up the people next door. If Bruff wakes up their baby . . ."

"I'll go and see what's the matter with him," said Rod.

"No, I'll go," his father said. "That's the end! If there's one thing I can't stand, it's a barking dog." He got up from his armchair.

Mr. Raven went to the door. Then he stopped. Bruff was growling now.

"And you can tell Jerry tomorrow morning that that dog's not to be here when I get home," Mr. Raven said. "He can ring up the Animal Rescue people first thing in the morning."

He went out. They heard the front door open and the sound of his footsteps. Bruff was quiet for a moment. Then he began growling again.

Jerry's head came round the door.

"Is that Bruff barking?" he asked.

Rod nodded.

At once Jerry dashed out of the front door. He had pulled on some clothes and was wide awake. He ran to the garage.

Rod jumped up and ran after him. But, as he went out of the front door, he saw Jerry racing out of the gate and into the street.

"What's up?" Rod asked his father who was standing in the half-opened garage door.

Mr. Raven did not reply.

By the light of the street lamp Rod saw a man at the other end of the garage. Bruff was standing in front of him. Rod could see the white of Bruff's teeth.

"Get him off me!" called the man.

Bruff growled.

"Call him off!" the man cried again.

Rod and his father did not move.

Then they saw the man begin to move slowly along the garage wall towards the door.

Bruff leapt forward and drove him back.

Rod saw the white teeth flash near the white face of the man.

"Get him off me! He'll tear me to bits!" the man called.

"Jerry's gone to ring for the police," Mr. Raven told Rod.

"I'll give myself up!" the man said. "Get this dog away from me."

"Shall I call Bruff?" Rod asked his father.

"No, don't call him," Jerry panted as he joined them at the garage door. "They're on their way, Dad," he said.

"Don't move," Jerry called to the man. "If you move he'll fly at you!"

The headlights of a car swept into the garage. The police-car came right up the short drive and stopped.

"Open the doors," said the policeman, as soon as he was out of the car.

When the doors were opened the car's headlights lit up the garage. Now they could see the man in the corner quite clearly. Bruff stood in front of him.

"Is that your dog?" asked the second policeman.

"He's mine!" Jerry told him.

"Call him off then," the policeman told him. "I don't want him going for me!" He wasn't joking.

"Bruff!" Jerry called.

Bruff's ears pricked up. He began to back slowly away from the man. All the time he kept his eyes on the man. Jerry slipped the lead round his neck.

"Come on out," ordered one of the policemen.

The two policemen went into the garage. One went down one side of Mr. Raven's car while the other policeman went down the other side. Jerry saw that they weren't taking any risks.

"We've been looking for you, Mister Fred York," said the policeman, as he snapped the hand-cuffs on.

Mr. Fred York was brought out of the garage. As he passed by Jerry, Bruff growled. The policemen put the man in the car. One of them got in next to him. The other policeman came back to where Mr. Raven was standing with Jerry and Rod. The police-car backed slowly into the street.

"It's a good job you caught him," said the policeman. "If you hadn't he'd have had your car in London to-night. By tomorrow morning he'd have sold it. We've been on the look-out for him. Odd. No one has even heard him before."

"It was the dog," explained Mr. Raven. "He was in the garage. We heard him bark."

"That explains it," said the policeman. "It's a boxer, isn't it? What was it doing in the garage?"

"He sleeps there," Jerry told him.

"He's a fine dog. He looks like a pedigree boxer to me," said the policeman. "I've always wanted one. You know what it is, Mr. Raven, we're out all hours. My wife and baby are on their own. They're wonderful guard dogs, boxers."

He bent down and stroked Bruff. At the same time he had a good look at the dog. "Of course," he went on, "if I had a dog like this I wouldn't put him in the garage. I'd have him in the house. Fine dog! Good with children, too."

"We've only just got him," said Mr. Raven.

"Yes," said the policeman. He got up. "We were going to come up and have a word with you, Mr. Raven."

"Oh," said Mr. Raven. "What about?"

"We had the farmer from Cross Farm ring up the station to-day. He said a boxer and a boy had been chasing his cows," said the policeman.

"That's a lie," said Jerry.

"Oh, it was you, was it?" said the policeman.

"The dog got out and I went to get him back," said Jerry hotly. "When I'd got Bruff away from the cows the farmer grabbed me. Bruff wasn't chasing them—he was just running round the field."

"So that was it," the policeman said with a smile.

"That's right," said Mr. Raven. "The farmer came to see me about it. I told him the dog hadn't been trained yet and that I'd see it didn't happen again."

"He said he'd shoot Bruff if he went there again," added Jerry. "And he must have stood there watching me trying to get Bruff. If he'd been so worried about his cows, why didn't he come and help me?"

"Perhaps he was as scared as our friend Mister Fred York," laughed the policeman. "Never mind, lad," he said to Jerry, "we'll call and see the farmer. Just to check up on this gun of his!"

"Well, thank you for coming so quickly," said Mr. Raven.

"Not at all," said the policeman. "I only wish everyone who called us had a boxer. It would make our job a lot simpler!"

The policeman got into the car.

"They've only had the boxer since yesterday!" he said to the policeman at the wheel of the police-car.

"You got him just in time!" said the police-car driver.

"Good-night, Mr. Raven. If you ever think of selling your boxer, just let me know," said the policeman.

"We won't be selling him," said Mr. Raven. "Good-night!"

The police-car pulled away into the night.

"It's gone cold," said Mr. Raven. "Go and get Bruff's bed and put it in the kitchen, Rod. That garage will be cold."

"Yes, Dad," said Rod and went off, grinning to himself.

"I take back all that I've said about Bruff, Jerry," Mr. Raven said.

"That's all right, Dad," said Jerry, with a smile.

They went back into the house. Jerry's mother wanted to know what had happened. Jerry and Rod said nothing. They wanted to hear their father tell the story about Bruff.

When he had told his wife, Mr. Raven said: "I was wrong. Bruff's just a young dog. He'll learn! But he's got guts. If it hadn't been for Bruff, we'd have lost the car. It's a good job we've got him."

Bruff was lying at Jerry's feet.

"Jerry will train him, won't you, Jerry?" said his mother.

"Yes," said Jerry. "But not too much! We don't want Bruff to become a lap-dog. Boxers have got lots of guts. I want to keep him that way!"

"Well," said his father, "just let me know if there's anything I can do. I want to do the right thing for Bruff."

"Thanks, Dad," grinned Jerry. "You could pay for the wire!"

"Good, I'll do that," his father agreed with a laugh.

"Fine," said Rod. "I'm saving up for a car now. Jill doesn't want me to have a motor-bike. . . ."

"That's a good thing," said his mother. "I've never wanted you to have a motor-bike, Rod. Jill's quite right. Now your father can teach you to drive the car!"

"The trouble these women make!" said Mr. Raven with a laugh.

"The trouble these dogs make!" said Jerry and Rod together.